*For the Ethiopian storytellers
of my childhood, and for my father,
whose stories made the longest night pass*
–J.K.

**To my sons,
Aaron and Joshua**
–E.B.L.

MAMO
ON
THE
MOUNTAIN

MAMO
ON
THE
MOUNTAIN

JANE KURTZ

ILLUSTRATED BY
E. B. LEWIS

GOLLANCZ CHILDREN'S PAPERBACKS
LONDON

In the high and beautiful mountains of Ethiopia there once lived a dreamer named Mamo. Day after day he wandered over the mountains with his uncle's sheep. While the sheep grazed, he would find a rock somewhere out of the wind where he could play his shepherd's flute and watch the birds and dream of flying. "Some day," he would say aloud to the sheep, "I will have a bag of money, and I will visit the faraway city of Gondar with its fine stone castles."

But his real life was hard; every day climbing over
the high mountain rocks in the high mountain wind and
guiding the sheep home every night. And it became harder
yet after both his mother and father died in one grim year
when disease swept through the village.

Then Mamo packed a small bag with some food,
an extra shirt and his shepherd's flute and set off to find
his sister, who was a cook in the house of a rich man.

He walked by waterfalls and watched baboons leap in the trees. He played his flute and dreamed his dreams. An ibis turned its black, black head to listen as Mamo passed.

For days he travelled ribbons of mountain paths until the road became broad and smooth and he knew he must be near the house of the rich man. While he was still a long way down the road, his sister ran out to meet him and kissed him on both cheeks and wept with him over the news he brought.

"Stay with me, little brother," she said, "and perhaps you can earn a few coins watching some of the rich man's cows."

So Mamo became a watcher of cows.
While he was watching the cows, he also
watched the rich man, who rode by every day
on his mule. Behind the mule walked a man
carrying the rich man's umbrella and behind him
walked seven servants with baskets of food on their
heads and behind them walked a young boy with a fly swish.
Every morning this procession went by and every night the
procession came back. But Mamo never heard the rich man
speak – until one day he came home in a fury.

That day Mamo heard him shouting a long way
off. "I am the master of my own household!" the man was
shouting. "I will not be insulted in the village!"

When Mamo brought the cows home that night,
the man was still shouting that someone in the village had
insulted him.

"Come," Mamo's sister whispered. "Help chop
the onions. Master is in a foul temper and wants to eat
immediately."

"Am I not as strong and brave as a lion?" the rich
man said, as the servants served him.

Not one of the servants said a word.

"Why, once I became lost in the cold mountains at night; but I leaned against my mule until morning and miraculously I survived to tell of it."

Suddenly he looked up from his food. "Tell me," he said, "have you ever heard of anyone else as strong or brave?"

All the servants but Mamo bowed their heads and went about their work. But Mamo said, "Many times when I watched my uncle's sheep, I, too, stayed in the cold air of the mountains throughout the night with only a thin cloak against the cold."

Rage choked the rich man's voice. "Are you trying to make me even angrier?"

"No, master," said Mamo. "I speak the truth."

The rich man looked around at all his servants. They did not appear to be listening, but he knew they were. "We'll see if you are telling the truth or lying," he said. "If you can do such a thing again, I will give you four cows and a bag of money besides. But you must take nothing to keep you warm but one thin *shemma*."

"Agreed," said Mamo.

"Not so fast." The rich man snorted. "Do not bite unless you are prepared to swallow. If you fail, you and your sister will be out of a job. You must leave my house and never come back."

The boy bowed his head. "Agreed," he whispered.

That evening Mamo's sister kissed him, and
Mamo set out with only a *shemma* wrapped around
him and his flute in his hand.

The rich man watched him go. "He will come crawling back in the middle of the night," the rich man said. "Or he will be stubborn and die of the cold up in the high mountains."

High in the mountains the wind danced and screamed through the rocks. At first Mamo played his flute, but the wind sang louder than the flute's song.

Night descended. The hyenas howled *oo-oo-oop* in the darkness. Mamo shivered and wrapped his *shemma* around his shoulders. But the wind bit his face and made him squint his eyes. The wind bit his feet and he could not tuck them far enough under his *shemma* to make them warm. The wind bit his hands where they clutched the cloak. He began to shiver so hard he could barely think. Even his dreams paled in the cold.

All night long the rich man ate and drank and talked of how strong he was, how brave. All night long he listened for the sound of Mamo crawling back. But he heard nothing. There was nothing to hear but the sound of his own boasting.

Then as morning light cracked the sky, he heard a shout. He rushed out of the house with the servants close behind.

There, in the morning fog, was Mamo's sister, pointing.

And there, emerging through the fog, was Mamo. "It was difficult, but I did as I said I would," the boy said.

The rich man shook his head. "Impossible," he spluttered.

"The night was bitter," Mamo said. "When all the sky was dark, I thought I would die. Then far, far off I saw a shepherd's fire on another mountain. I kept my eyes on the red glow in the distance, and I dreamed of being warm. And that is how I had the strength to survive."

"Hah!" the rich man shouted. He puffed out his chest like a huge drum. "You lose the cows and the bag of money. You and your sister can start packing your belongings."

"Why?" the servants protested.

"Looking at a fire on the mountain is the same as building a fire," gloated the rich man. "I knew the boy could not make it through the night with only a thin cloak to protect him."

He clapped his hands. "Prepare a great feast!" he told the servants. Then he turned to Mamo. "You may stay to celebrate my victory; but by tomorrow morning, you and your sister must be gone."

Mamo bowed his head and went to his sister's room to get warm, but the other servants whispered behind their master's back.

All that day the whispers ran like water through the rich man's house. As for Mamo and his sister, they stayed in the room with their heads close together, talking.

That night when the rich man arrived home, he saw his servants carrying stacks of whitest, finest *injera*. From the kitchen behind the house came smells of *wat* of all kinds. The man rubbed his hands. His stomach rumbled.

After he and his friends were seated at the *mesob*, a servant brought water so they could wash their hands. The smells grew as strong as loud music, but no food was brought to the great basket.

Finally, the master waved to a nearby servant. "Here! Can't you see we are tired of waiting? Play us some music on the *krar* to make the minutes pass."

The servant lifted his *krar*. His fingers began to move, but not once did they touch the strings.

At last Mamo's sister arrived and bowed low. "I hope you have enjoyed your fine meal," she said to the master and his guests. "We prepared all your favourite foods tonight and played the best music."

"But we have had no food!" the man shouted. "We have had no music."

"Ah, but you smelled food all evening. You heard your favourite music in your mind. Is that not enough?"

"Enough?" The man howled with rage. "What kind of person thinks that smells of food can fill a man's stomach?"

Mamo's sister smiled. "The same kind of person who believes that looking at a fire can keep a boy warm."

All the servants and the master's guests as well began to laugh behind their hands.

The rich man darkened with anger. But the next morning, without a word, he got the bag of money and the cows and gave them to Mamo.

From that day on, Mamo tended his own cows
and they eventually became a great herd. Then Mamo,
too, rode his mule out every morning. His servants
walked behind in a great procession, laughing and talking
with baskets of food on their heads. When they reached
the village each day, Mamo spread the food for everyone
to share. His sister lived in his house and became even
wiser as she grew older so that people came to her for
advice from the neighbouring villages, from the faraway city
of Gondar, and from all of Ethiopia and beyond.

AUTHOR'S NOTE

As a child growing up in Ethiopia, I heard this story a number of times.
The story, in fact, is known in many forms on almost every continent
in the world. Mamo's sister does not appear in the version that I heard as
a child. There is, however, a tradition of strong women in Ethiopian stories.
The most famous, of course, is the Queen of Sheba, who, according to a
very old Ethiopian story, travelled across the Red Sea from Ethiopia to the
land of Israel, where she dazzled King Solomon with her beauty and wisdom.

First published in the USA in 1994
by Simon & Schuster Books for Young Readers

First published in Great Britain
in Gollancz Children's Paperbacks 1995
by Victor Gollancz
A Division of the Cassell group
Wellington House, 125 Strand, London WC2R 0BB

A catalogue record for this book is
available from the British Library

ISBN 0 575 05991 5

Printed in Hong Kong by Wing King Tong Co. Ltd.